# THE
# POKY LITTLE PUPPY

*by*

JANETTE SEBRING LOWREY

*illustrated by*

GUSTAF TENGGREN

A GOLDEN BOOK • NEW YORK
Western Publishing Company, Inc., Racine, Wisconsin 53404

FIVE little puppies dug a hole under the
fence and went for a walk in the wide, wide
world.

Through the meadow they went, down
the road, over the bridge, across the green
grass, and up the hill, one after the other.

And when they got to the top of the hill, they counted themselves: one, two, three, four. One little puppy wasn't there.

"Now where in the world is that poky little puppy?" they wondered. For he certainly wasn't on top of the hill.

He wasn't going down the other side. The
only thing they could see going down was a
fuzzy caterpillar.

He wasn't coming up this side. The only
thing they could see coming up was a quick
green lizard.

But when they looked down at the grassy place near the bottom of the hill, there he was, running round and round, his nose to the ground.

"What is he doing?" the four little puppies asked one another. And down they went to see, roly-poly, pell-mell, tumble-bumble, till they came to the green grass; and there they stopped short.

"What in the world are you doing?" they asked.

"I smell something!" said the poky little puppy.

Then the four little puppies began to sniff, and they smelled it, too.

"Rice pudding!" they said.

And home they went, as fast as they could go, over the bridge, up the road, through the meadow, and under the fence. And there, sure enough, was dinner waiting for them, with rice pudding for dessert.

But their mother was greatly displeased. "So you're the little puppies who dig holes under fences!" she said. "No rice pudding tonight!" And she made them go straight to bed.

But the poky little puppy came home after everyone was sound asleep.

He ate up the rice pudding and crawled into bed as happy as a lark.

The next morning someone had filled the hole and put up a sign. The sign said:

BUT. . . . .

The five little puppies dug a hole under the fence, just the same, and went for a walk in the wide, wide world.

Through the meadow they went, down the road, over the bridge, across the green grass, and up the hill, two and two. And when they got to the top of the hill, they counted themselves: one, two, three, four. One little puppy wasn't there.

"Now where in the world is that poky little puppy?" they wondered. For he certainly wasn't on top of the hill.

He wasn't going down the other side. The only thing they could see going down was a big black spider.

He wasn't coming up this side. The only thing they could see coming up was a brown hop-toad.

But when they looked down at the grassy place near the bottom of the hill, there was the poky little puppy, sitting still as a stone, with his head on one side and his ears cocked up.

"What is he doing?" the four little puppies asked one another. And down they went to see, roly-poly, pell-mell, tumble-bumble, till they came to the green grass; and there they stopped short.

"What in the world are you doing?" they asked.

"I hear something!" said the poky little puppy.

The four little puppies listened, and they could hear it, too. "Chocolate custard!" they cried. "Someone is spooning it into our bowls!"

And home they went as fast as they could go, over the bridge, up the road, through the meadow, and under the fence. And there, sure enough, was dinner waiting for them, with chocolate custard for dessert.

But their mother was greatly displeased. "So you're the little puppies who will dig holes under fences!" she said. "No chocolate custard tonight!" And she made them go straight to bed.

But the poky little puppy came home after everyone else was sound asleep, and he ate up all the chocolate custard and crawled into bed as happy as a lark.

The next morning someone had filled the hole and put up a sign.

The sign said:

DON'T EVER **EVER** DIG HOLES UNDER THIS FENCE!

BUT...

In spite of that, the five little puppies dug a hole under the fence and went for a walk in the wide, wide world.

Through the meadow they went, down the road, over the bridge, across the green grass, and up the hill, two and two. And when they got to the top of the hill, they counted themselves: one, two, three, four. One little puppy wasn't there.

"Now where in the world is that poky little puppy?" they wondered. For he certainly wasn't on top of the hill.

He wasn't going down the other side. The only thing they could see going down was a little grass snake.

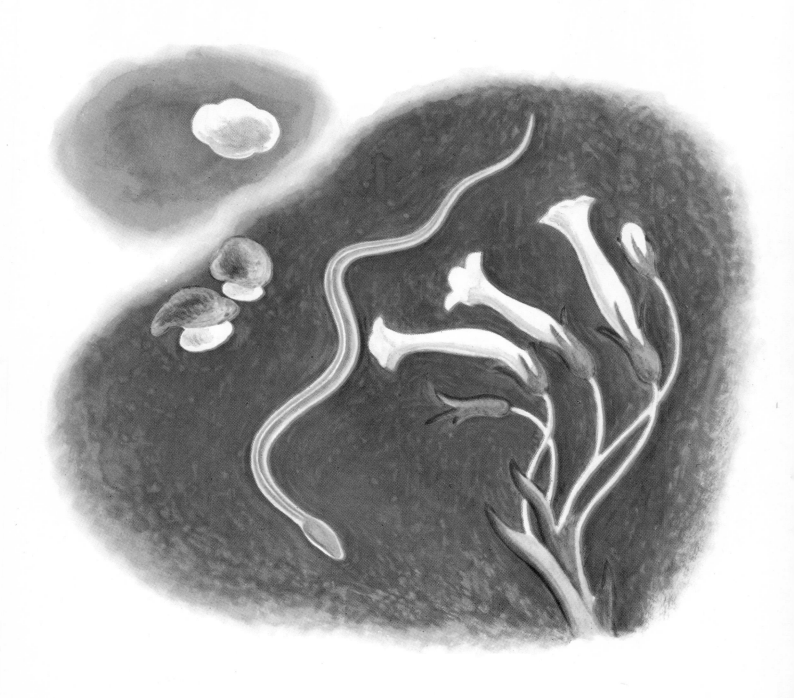

He wasn't coming up this side. The only thing they could see coming up was a big grasshopper.

But when they looked down at the grassy place near the bottom of the hill, there he was, looking hard at something on the ground in front of him.

"What is he doing?" the four little puppies asked one another. And down they went to see, roly-poly, pell-mell, tumble-bumble, till they came to the green grass; and there they stopped short.

"What in the world are you doing?" they asked.

"I see something!" said the poky little puppy.

The four little puppies looked, and they could see it, too. It was a ripe, red strawberry growing there in the grass.

"Strawberry shortcake!" they cried.

And home they went as fast as they could go, over the bridge, up the road, through the meadow, and under the fence. And there, sure enough, was dinner waiting for them, with strawberry shortcake for dessert.

But their mother said: "So you're the little puppies who dug that hole under the fence again! No strawberry shortcake for supper tonight!" And she made them go straight to bed.

But the four little puppies waited till they thought she was asleep, and then they slipped out and filled up the hole, and when they turned around, there was their mother watching them.

"What good little puppies!" she said. "Come have some strawberry shortcake!"

And this time, when the poky little puppy got home, he had to squeeze in through a wide place in the fence. And there were his four brothers and sisters, licking the last crumbs from their saucer.

"Dear me!" said his mother. "What a pity you're so poky! Now the strawberry shortcake is all gone!"

So poky little puppy had to go to bed without a single bite of shortcake, and he felt very sorry for himself.

And the next morning someone had put up a sign that read:

NO DESSERTS EVER
UNLESS PUPPIES NEVER
DIG HOLES UNDER THIS
FENCE AGAIN !

# THE
# GINGERBREAD MAN

# The Gingerbread Man

## Illustrated by Bonnie and Bill Rutherford

A GOLDEN BOOK • NEW YORK
Western Publishing Company, Inc.
Racine, Wisconsin 53404

Once long ago in a little old house lived a little old man and a little old woman.

The little old woman worked in the house all day, polishing and dusting and baking wonderful cakes and pies and cookies.

The little old man worked all day in the garden. In the evening he ate the wonderful cakes and pies and cookies that the little old woman had baked.

One day the little old woman said to herself, "What can I bake for a surprise? I am tired of the same old cakes and pies and cookies....I know, I'll bake a gingerbread man!"

Carefully she cut out the gingerbread man. She used two lavender gumdrops for his eyes, a licorice drop for his nose, and a red candy heart for his mouth. She put peppermint-drop buttons on his jacket and made a hat of mint green sugar. Oh, he was a lovely gingerbread man!

When she had placed him in the oven she hummed a little song, thinking of the old man's delight when he saw his surprise.

After a bit, the little old woman opened the door of the oven to see if the gingerbread man was ready. Swish! Out he jumped! He laughed and ran right across the kitchen.

"Stop!" cried the little old woman. "You are to be a surprise! We want to eat you!"

But the gingerbread man laughed and said, "I am the gingerbread man, I am! I can run, I can, I can!" And he ran

out the door and past the little old man in the garden.

Up jumped the little old man. "Stop! I want to eat you, gingerbread man!" he shouted as he ran after the little old woman who was chasing the gingerbread man.

But the gingerbread man just laughed. "I am the ginger-bread man, I am! I can run, I can, I can!" And the little old man and the little old woman soon became tired and gave up the chase.

The gingerbread man kept running down the lane. Soon he saw a brown cow grazing in the shade. The cow twitched her tail when she saw him.

"Stop, gingerbread man! I want to eat you!" the cow mooed.

But the gingerbread man just laughed and ran faster. "I am the gingerbread man, I am! I can run, I can, I can! I ran away from an old woman and an old man, and I can run from you, too, old cow, I can, I can!"

Soon the cow grew tired of running, but the gingerbread
man kept on.

After a while he passed a large black horse rolling in a field. The horse looked surprised to see a runaway gingerbread man.

"Stop! I want to eat you!" he neighed.

But the gingerbread man just laughed and said, "I am the gingerbread man, I am! I can run, I can, I can! I ran away from an old woman and an old man, and from a cow, too, and I can run away from you, I can, I can!"

He soon left the horse far behind him.

Pretty soon he met a yellow cat sunning herself in a daisy patch. "Stop! I want to eat you!" the cat mewed hungrily.

But the gingerbread man just laughed and boasted, "I am the gingerbread man, I am! I can run, I can, I can! I ran away from a little old woman and a little old man, a brown cow and a black horse, too, and I can easily run away from you! Yes, I can!"

The gingerbread man ran faster. The cat ran after him until she saw another daisy patch, and being very tired, she lay down in the sun again. Then, just ahead of him, the gingerbread man saw a river. A red fox was sitting on the bank, blinking in the sun.

"Hello, gingerbread man," said the red fox. "Are you going across the river? I've just finished a *huge* dinner and I am about to swim back to my home on the other side. Would you like to ride on my back?"

The gingerbread man thought about it. Surely it would be all right, since the fox said he had just finished his dinner.

"I'll climb up on your tail," the gingerbread man decided. *That should be safe enough,* he thought.

"Of course," agreed the fox. He jumped into the sparkling river. "It's getting a little deep now," he said. "Maybe you had better climb up on my back—just to keep dry, of course."

The gingerbread man climbed up on the fox's back.

*That should be safe enough,* he thought.

"Oh, my, it's really deep now," said the fox as he swam along. "Maybe you'd better climb up on top of my head, gingerbread man!"

And so the gingerbread man did just that.

"Oops, be careful," said the fox. "I think you'd better climb on my nose so you won't fall off!"

The gingerbread man reminded himself that the fox had just eaten a very large dinner. He climbed onto the fox's nose and—POP! That sly old fox gobbled the gingerbread man right up!

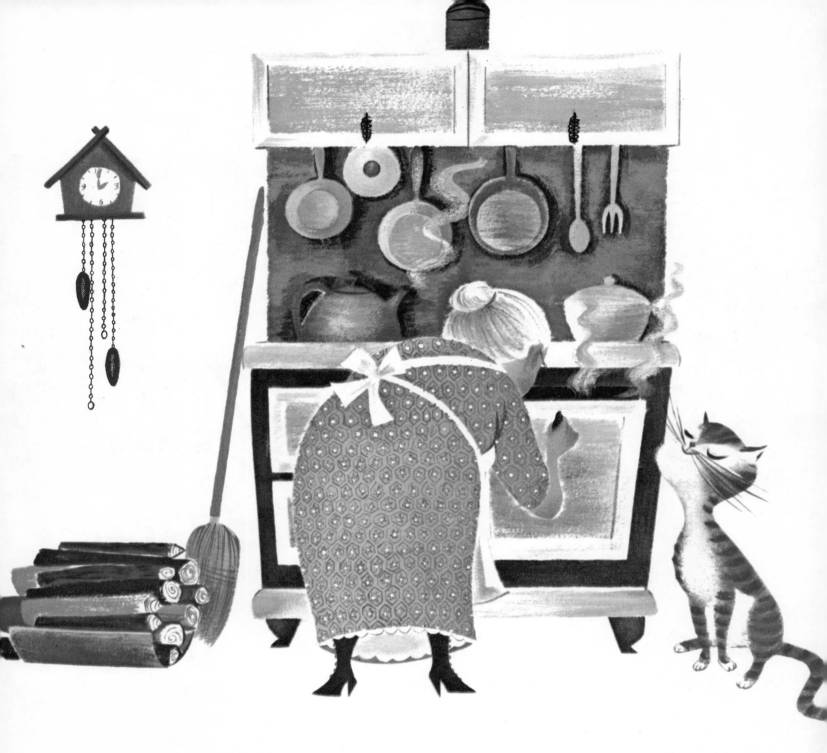

Now that was the very last gingerbread man ever to come down the lane past the cow and the horse and the cat and the fox. For the next time the little old lady baked a gingerbread man she was careful to keep the oven door closed until the little old man was all ready for his very special surprise.

# The Little
# Red Caboose

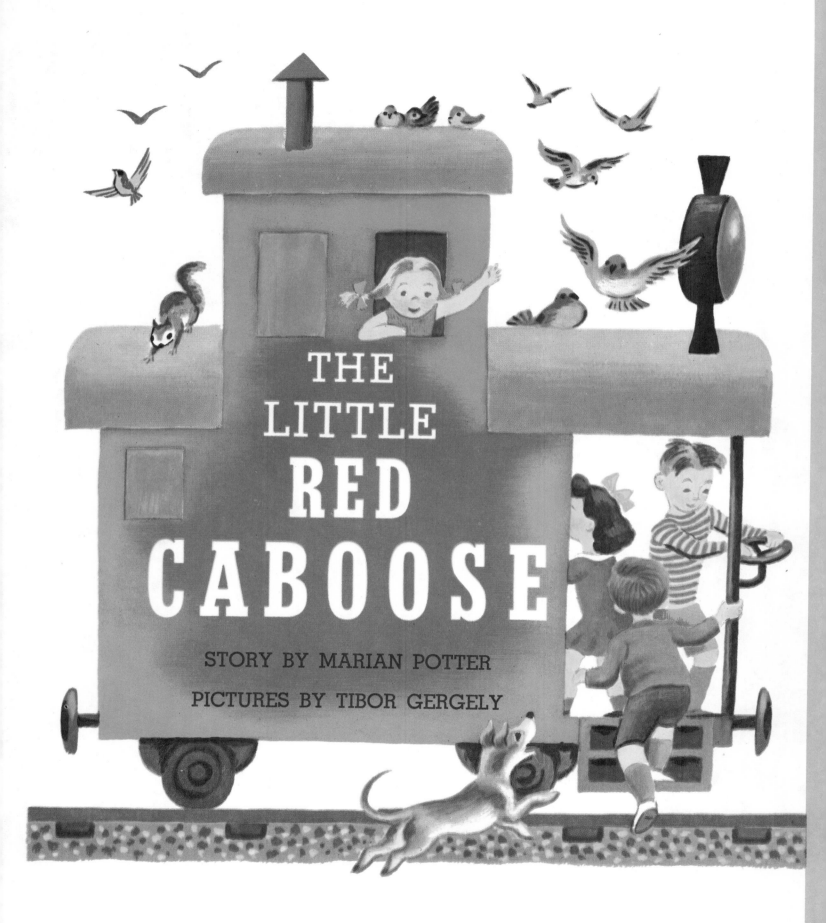

# THE LITTLE RED CABOOSE

STORY BY MARIAN POTTER

PICTURES BY TIBOR GERGELY

A GOLDEN BOOK • NEW YORK
Western Publishing Company, Inc., Racine, Wisconsin 53404

FOR ANDREW, PAMELA, AND REBECCA

The little red caboose
always came last.

First came the big black engine,
puffing and chuffing.

Then came the boxcars,

then the oil cars,

then the coal cars,

then the flat cars.
Sometimes they were
switched around in different ways.

But the little red caboose
always came last.

Boys and girls waved
at the big black engine.

They listened to the boxcars
and the oil cars
and the coal cars
and the flat cars
go *clickety clack.*

But by the time the little red caboose
came along, the boys and girls
were turning away.
Because the little red caboose
always came last.

"Oh, smoke!" said the little red caboose.
"I wish I were a flat car
or a coal car or an oil car
or a boxcar, so boys and
girls would wave at me.

"How I wish I were a big black engine,
puffing and chuffing way up
at the front of the train!

"But I'm just the little old red caboose.
Nobody cares for me."

One day the train
started up a mountain.
   Up went the big black engine.
   Up went the boxcars.
   Up went the oil cars.
   Up went the coal cars.
   Up went the flat cars.
   Up went the little red caboose.
   "Hang on tight, little caboose,"
called the flat car.
"This is a long tall mountain.
And you are the last car
on the train."

"Don't I know it!"
sighed the little red caboose.
"Poor me!"
  The train went slower
and slower and s-l-o-w-e-r.
  Soon it was hardly moving.
  It looked as if that train
could not get up the mountain.

"Look out, little caboose!"
called the flat car.
"The train is starting to slip
back down this long tall mountain!"
"Not if I can help it!"
said the little red caboose.

And he slammed on his brakes.
And he held tight to the tracks.
And he kept that train
from sliding down the mountain!

Then, *bump!* The little red caboose
felt something push him from behind.
It was two big black engines.
They pushed the train up to the top
of the mountain.

"We couldn't have done it,"
said the big black engines,
"if it had not been for the
little red caboose."
Everyone cheered.
And the little red caboose
nearly burst with pride.

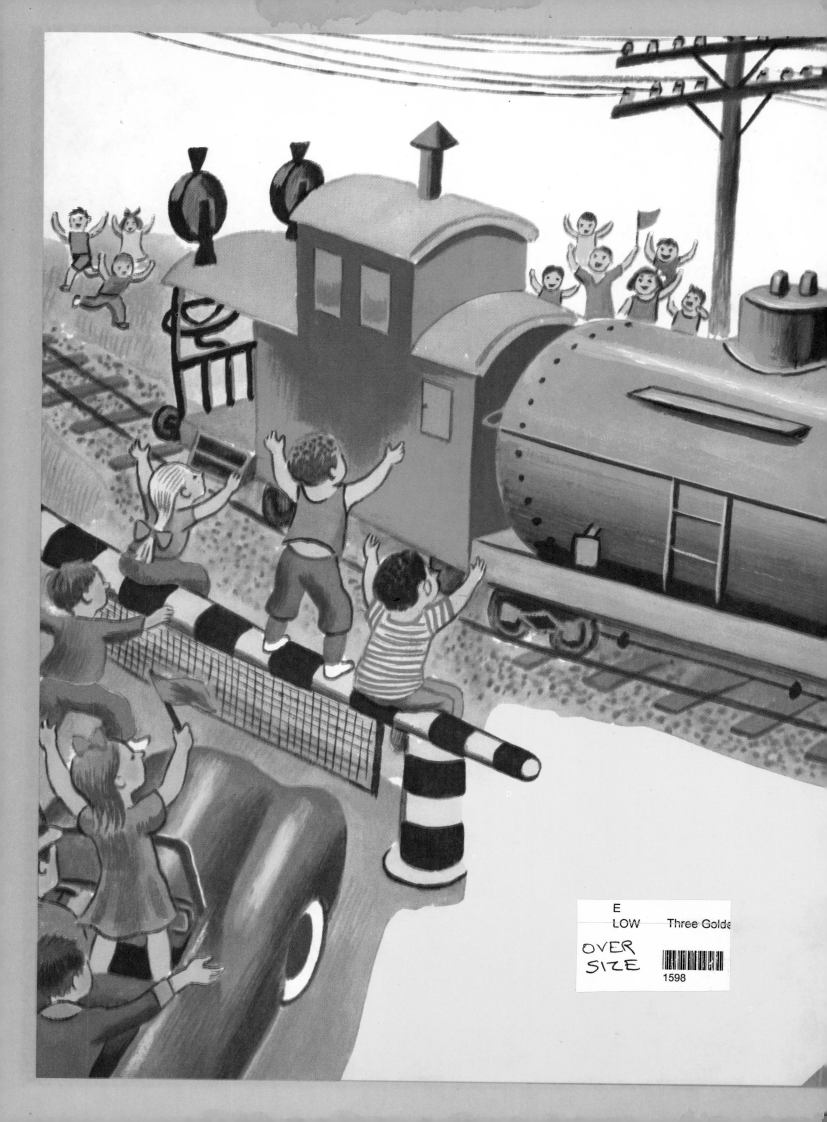